THEY CALL ME GÜERO

A BORDER KID'S POEMS

by DAVID BOWLES

El Paso . Tejas

"Border Kid" first appeared in *Here We Go: A Poetry Friday Power Book (*Princeton, NJ: Pomelo Books, 2017), edited by Sylvia Vardell and Janet Wong. It was then reprinted in the *Journal of Children's Literature*, 43(1), p. 16, 2017.

FIRST EDITION
10 9 8 7 6 5 4 3 2

Library of Congress Cataloging-in-Publication Data

Names: Bowles, David (David O.), author.
Title: They call me Guero : a border kid's poems / David Bowles.
Description: First edition. | El Paso, Texas : Cinco Puntos Press, [2018] |
Summary: Twelve-year-old Guero, a red-headed, freckled Mexican American border kid, discovers the joy of writing poetry, thanks to his seventh grade English teacher.
Identifiers: LCCN 2018027137| ISBN 978-1-947627-06-2 (cloth : alk. cloth)
ISBN 978-1-947627-07-9 (paper)
Subjects: | CYAC: Novels in verse. | Mexican Americans—Fiction. | Poetry—Fiction.
Classification: LCC PZ7.5.B69 Th 2018 | DDC [Fic]—dc23
LC record available at https://lccn.loc.gov/2018027137

Designed by Michelle Lange, Whack Publications
Front and back cover illustrations by Zeke Peña, zpvisual.com | @zpvisual
Moving up with the big boys in Boston now. Don't forget home.

CONTENTS

To my family, friends, teachers, and community—
without you, I am nothing.

BORDER KID

It's fun to be a border kid, to wake up early Saturdays
and cross the bridge to Mexico with my dad.

The town's like a mirror twin of our own,
with Spanish spoken everywhere just the same
but English mostly missing till it pops up
like grains of sugar on a chili pepper.

We have breakfast in our favorite restorán.
Dad sips café de olla while I drink chocolate—
then we walk down uneven sidewalks, chatting
with strangers and friends in both languages.

Later we load our car with Mexican cokes and Joya,
avocados and cheese, tasty reminders of our roots.

Waiting in line at the bridge, though, my smile fades.
The border fence stands tall and ugly, invading
the carrizo at the river's edge. Dad sees me staring,
puts his hand on my shoulder. "Don't worry, m'ijo:

"You're a border kid, a foot on either bank.
Your ancestors crossed this river a thousand times.
No wall, no matter how tall, can stop your heritage
from flowing forever, like the Río Grande itself."

BORDERLANDS

Sixty miles wide
on either side
of the river,
my people's home
stretches from gulf
to mountain pass.
These borderlands,
strip of frontier,
home of hardy plants.
The thorn forest
with its black willows,
Texas ebony, mesquite,
huisache and brasil.
Transplanted fields
of corn and onion,
sorghum and sugarcane.
Foreign orchards
of ruby red grapefruit
white with flowers.
Native brush
rainbow bright
with purple sage,
rock rose, manzanilla
and hackberry fruit.
Beyond its edges spreads
the wild desert,
harsh and lovely
like a barrel cactus
in sunny bloom.

CHECKPOINT

On our road trip to San Antonio
for shopping and Six Flags,
Dad slows the car as we approach
the checkpoint, all those border patrol
in their green uniforms, guns on their belts.
Mom clutches los papeles—our passports,
her green card. She's from Mexico. A resident,
not a citizen, by her own choice. At the checkpoint
a giant German Shepherd sniffs the tires
as the agents ask questions, inspect our trunk.
My little brother squeezes my hand, afraid.
My rebel sister nods and says her yessirs,
but I can tell she's mad, the way her eyes get.
We're innocent, sure, but our hearts beat fast.

We've heard stories.
Bad stories.

A cold nod and we're waved along,
allowed to leave the borderlands—
made a limbo by the uncaring laws
of people a long way away who don't know us,
a quarantine zone between white and brown.
I feel angry, just like my sister,
but I hold it tight inside.

We just don't understand
why we have to prove every time
that we belong in our own country
where our mother gave birth to us.
Dad, like he can feel the bad vibes
coming from the back seat, tells us to chill.

"It won't always be like this," he says,
"but it's up to us to make the change,
especially los jóvenes, you and your friends.
Eyes peeled. Stay frosty. Learn and teach the truth.
Right now? What matters is San Antonio.
We'll take your mom shopping,
go swimming in the Texas-shaped pool,
and eat a big dinner at Tito's.
Order anything you want."

And he slides his favorite CD
into the battered radio. Los Tigres del Norte
start belting out "La Puerta Negra"—

"Pero ni la puerta ni cien candados
van a poder detenerme."

Not the door. Not one hundred locks.
Ah, my dad. He always knows the right song.

OUR HOUSE

Our house wasn't ready all at once.
Our house took years to grow,
like a Monterrey oak gone from acorn
to tall and broad and shady tree.

My parents saved for years,
bought a nice lot on the edge of town,
drew up the plans with Tío Mike.

One year the family poured the foundation,
then the next these concrete walls went up.
At last my father built a sturdy roof,
and in we moved,
finishing it room by room,
everyone lending a hand,
every spare penny spent
para hacernos un hogar—
a home that glows warm with love.

Now it's like a bit of our souls
has fused with the block and wood.
I can't imagine life without this place—
on these tiles I learned to walk.
Here are my height marks,
with fading dates,
higher and higher.
Oh, all the laughs and tears

we've shared at that table!
All the cool movies we've watched
sitting on that couch!

And here's my room,
filled with all my favorite stuff,
sitting in the shade of the anacua tree
I once helped to plant.

A modest home, sure,
but inside its cozy walls we celebrate
all the riches that matter.

PULGA PANTOUM

Mom and I love to go to the pulga,
to get lost in the crowd that flows
between all the busy stalls,
drawn to colors, sounds, and smells.

To get lost in the crowd. That flows
from our instincts, I bet. Humans are
drawn to colors, sounds, and smells
like a swarm of bees to blooming flowers.

From our instincts, I bet humans are
happiest together. Bulging bags in hand,
like a swarm of bees to blooming flowers,
people meet for friendly haggling.

Happiest together, bulging bags in hand—
Mom and I love to go to the pulga!
People meet for friendly haggling
between all the busy stalls.

FINGERS & KEYS

My mom's the organist
for our parish—
One of the last, she says.

When I was little, she taught me to play
on a worn-out old upright
that stands in a corner
of our dining room,
holding up family photos.

Even though I'm twelve now,
when I sit down to practice,
laying my hands
upon the keys,
I sometimes feel her fingers on mine
light as feathers
but guiding me
all the same.

LULLABY

Like lots of border kids,
my first song was a lullaby
that my abuela sang
to warn me and to mystify.

My mom says when I got home,
smiling without teeth,
she took me in her arms
and serenaded me—

Duérmete mi niño
duérmeteme ya
porque viene el Cucu
y te comerá.

Go to sleep, my baby
sleep for me right now
to keep Cucu from coming
and swallowing you down.

Y si no te come,
él te llevará
hasta su casita
que en el monte está.

And if he doesn't eat you
he'll take you far from me
to his little cabin
that sits amid the trees.

So I learned the dangers
of this crazy, mixed-up place—
there are monsters lurking,
but family lore can keep you safe.

LEARNING TO READ

When I was a little kid,
my abuela Mimi would ease down
into her old, creaky rocking chair
to tell my cousins and me
such spine-tingling tales
as ever a pingo fronterizo,
crazy for cucuys, could hope to hear.

I always had questions
at the end of Mimi's stories.
What was the little boy's name?
What did his parents do
when they found him missing
from his room?
Is there a special police squad
that tracks down monster hands
and witch owls and sobbing spirits
in order to save the boys and girls
that they've stolen?

"No sé, m'ijo. The story just ends.
Happened once upon a time.
Nobody knows."
But I didn't get it. I was so literal.
I believed every story she told was true.
So I kept asking my questions,

guessing at answers
till she broke down at last
and told me the greatest truth:
"You have to learn to read, Güerito.
You will only find what you seek
in the pages of books."

So I began to bug my mom
to teach me to read till she did.
I was barely five at the time.
First day of kinder arrived, and I was so excited
at all the books my sister said were waiting
on the shelves for me.
But then the teacher started drawing
the letter "A" on the board, and I soon got it—
none of the other kids could read.
She was going to teach us the alphabet
one letter per day! Not me! No way!
I dropped out of kindergarten,
little rebel that I was.

Instead, my mom took me
to the public library
every day, all year long.
I read book after book after book
delighting in the new tales,
the strange and mysterious places.

And when first grade rolled around
(not optional like kinder),
the school was so amazed at my skill
they put me in a third-grade reading class!
I got picked on, sure, but I was pretty proud
and didn't care when kids called me nerd.

The school counselor told my folks
I can already read at college level!
And I've found lots of answers,
but also many new questions.
Of course I pass all the state tests
with super high scores.
Learning in class is easy for me.
Dad says all those books
rewired my brain,
got me ready
for study.

Just think—
I owe it all to those stories
my abuelita used to tell us
sitting in her rocking chair
as we shivered and thrilled.
Even then, words were burrowing
into my brain and waiting,
like larvae in a chrysalis,
to unfold their paper wings
and take me flying into the future.

NAGUAL

Late one summer night
at the ranch,
we all gather 'round the fire
as the dark wraps around us,
Uncle Joe tells us of the nagual—
magical trickster shaman
who shakes off his human form
to reveal the beast within—
coyote, wolf or dog—
and raids ranches
to feast on cows and sheep.

Wow!

I wish I knew that magic,
could say some spell
or perform some ritual
so I could slip my skin
like that fabled shapeshifter
and feel the freedom,
running beneath the stars,
night wind in my fur,
eyes bright with glints
of moonlight
and wild animal joy!

BOTTLE ROCKET BATTLE

Like every other Fourth of July,
we gather to celebrate out on the ranch.
My father and uncles light the mesquite
as they sip on cervezas and talk about sports.

While our mothers prepare the feast,
my cousins and brother shoot BBs at birds.
But Teresa and me, we just huddle inside
and enjoy a new video, laughing at jokes.

Our abuela's invited the new parish priest:
He flies back and forth like a black Chachalaca.
I guess it gets boring hearing confession,
so now he's all busy, sharing the gossip!

When the carne asada is ready, we eat.
I stuff quesadillas with fajitas and beans,
guacamole as well. Then I grab a coke
from the ice. It's apple, my favorite flavor.

The music is loud, lots of cumbias and salsa
streamed from our Tía Isabel's phone,
mixing with laughter and shouts and singing
as the sleepy red sun slips its way from the sky.

Soon it gets dark. Since our bellies are full,
all us kids group together and open the fireworks.
The little huerquitos get bags of snapdragons.
Others light strings of black cats and laugh.

Now Grandpa Manuel, a Vietnam vet,
gives a moving speech about the U.S.,
the country he loves, the friends he lost,
and his dreams for us all. A moment of silence.

Then Isabel pulls up Grandpa's favorite playlist,
and to the beat of patriotic songs,
Uncle Joe and Tío Mike
set off the bigger, brighter bangs!

The national anthem fades. Then sparklers slash
the dark in the hands of pingos, like Jedi
who face a horde of deadly Sith.
My cousin René gives a sinful grin.

"Are you ready for bottle rocket battle?"
he asks us older boys with a wave.
We all nod and follow as he leads us behind
his father's stable. We gasp and cheer.

That René, he has taken plastic pipe,
electrician's tape and bits of wood,
and made six weapons, one for each.
"These are bottle rocket rifles," he says.

He shows us how to shoot them, to slide in the rocket,
wedge the fuse tight at the mouth of the pipe.
We flick our fathers' lighters with glee,
quickly scattering to take deadly aim!

I dodge the missile that Joseph lets fly:
It explodes far away, flinging its sparks.
Timoteo, however, is struck in the chest
by Raúl's perfect aim! WHOOSH! BAM!

It's war! We rush through the brush with whoops,
a half dozen rockets shoved in back pockets.
HISS! René's deadly dart whizzes right by,
singeing the back of my hair! OW!

Soon the battle invades the grown-ups' domain.
All the men start grinning and egging us on,
though our mothers shout angry rebukes:
"¡Muchachos traviesos, se van a lastimar!"

But it's not us who get hurt that night.
Clumsy me, I stumble as I lift my weapon:
With a screaming whistle, the rocket hits
the ground and hurtles toward Father García...

OH, NO! It strikes his foot and shoots up his pant leg,
exploding right above his knee. BOOM!
Oh, the squeal that he lets loose! YOWL!

The sound still echoes in my ears as I work my way
through the long list of chores my angry mother
has dreamed up for the rest of my summer.

FIRST DAY OF SEVENTH GRADE

Khakis, uniform shirt, belt—
you'd think I'd hate
going back to middle school,
but I'm super excited!

See, I hang with an unusual crowd.
Bobby Handy, the half-white Chicano;
Bobby Lee, whose parents are from Seoul;
and Bobby Delgado, dominicano moreno.

I think of us as el Güero y los Bobbys,
like we're some famous Tejano band.
My sister Teresa calls us los Derds—Diverse
Nerds. We like comics, gaming, and books.

It seems like forever
since I've seen my three friends,
all busy with family this summer—
least we had Snapchat and Skype!

Dad drops me off, though I'd rather walk.
Los Bobbys are already in the cafeteria
grabbing breakfast. Fist bumps
all around. We smile and insult each other.

We compare schedules. Just a few
shared classes, but we'll meet
in the library like always.
The bell rings. We're off!

It's like navigating down the
Río Grande, avoiding the lockers,
steering through the middle channel.
I get to homeroom, and lucky me.

Snake Barrera. The bully.
Looks like he's fifteen.
My dad once fired his dad.
Now he hates my guts.

But my teachers are woke,
especially for English and band,
and a girl in social studies
glances at me twice.

When I catch her looking,
she smirks and shakes her head.
My stomach flops, and I'm shook—
I think it's going to be a great year.

LOS BOBBYS, OR THE BOOKWORM SQUAD

If we were a team
of super heroes,
this would be
our origin story.

It was last year.
Sixth grade.
Middle school's
kind of a shock,
especially for nerdy
little border kids.
All the tall guys
almost like grown-ups,
all the girls, even taller,
traveling in scary
Amazon groups.

I ended up
in the library.
Every day.
Before school
and during lunch.
One day, Bobby Handy
walked in. Finally
someone I knew!

We sat together,
reading and sharing
clever lines
or plot points.

After a few weeks,
we noticed another
couple of loners
creeping around
in the dusty corners
of the non-fiction
section. I approached,
introduced myself.

Bobby Handy almost
passed out laughing
when they said their names:
Roberto Delgado
and Robert Lee.
"Three Bobbys,"
I explained as they stared.
"And one Güero,"
Handy managed to add.

Here's the mentor part.
All heroes need one.
Mr. Soria, the librarian,
all bushy hair and eyebrows,
came over to shush us.

But within a few minutes
of weird questions,
he figured out what
major nerds we are.

"Let's talk about books,"
he suggested. "Cool ones.
I'll show you the best."
He was freaky and funny
and pretty persuasive.

That was the birth of
the Bookworm Squad.
Now we come together
twice a day
to swap favorite titles
and look for new greats.

Lucky us! Mr. Soria knows
all sorts of writers who look
and talk like us: Dominicans,
Koreans, Mexicans, Chicanos,
Black and Native folks, too.

It's the perfect time for us,
for diverse nerds and geeks,
for all woke readers—
heroes whose power
is traveling through these pages
to distant times and places
to find our proud reflections.

THEY CALL ME GÜERO

In my family, I have the lightest skin.
My big sister Teresa is toasty brown
and little Arturo's the color of honey.
But I'm pasty white, covered in freckles.

Everyone's got a nickname for me—
Tío Danny calls me El Pecas, while
Grandpa Manuel tussles my copper hair
and shouts, "Way to go, Red!"

Most folks? They call me Güero.
In fact they use that word so much
that when I was a little squirt,
I thought it was my name!

My family loves my paleness,
even Teresa, who says she's jealous.
I look like my grandmother,
lots of Spanish and Irish blood.

But at school, it's a different story,
as if my complexion's on purpose.
The haters say I think I'm all that,
call me "el Canelo chafo" and laugh.

Their taunts make me wish I could box
like Saúl Álvarez, the real Canelo—
my hands ache to curl into fists
and pound my problems away.

But I swallow my pride, keep calm.
When Dad picks me up, he can tell.
"What's wrong, Güero? Looks like
you're ready to punch someone."

As he drives, I explain, jaw tight.
My dad puts his hand on mine.
It's deep brown like mesquite bark
or clay from Mexican soil.

I wish my skin were like that
not all pink and freckled,
turning lobster red in the border sun
to match my rusty hair.

"M'ijo, pale folks catch all the breaks
here and in Mexico, too. Not your fault.
Not fair. Just the way it's been for years.
Doors will open for you that won't for me."

My eyes fill with tears. "But I didn't ask
anyone to open them for me!"

Dad squeezes my hand. "No, but now
you've got to hold them open for us all."

MS. WONG & THE RABBIT

This year, my English teacher
opens up a whole new world to me.

I can tell right away that Ms. Wong
will be different. For example—

she has a white rabbit in her room: Nun.
White, with floppy ears. A "lop," she says.

(Bobby Lee says "Nun" means "snow" and
"Eye" in Korean—the bunny's eyes are red.)

The first week of school, Ms. Wong talks about
the Moon Rabbit. In both Korea and Mexico,

people have long believed the marks on the moon
are the shape of a rabbit, placed there by the gods.

We read Aztec and Maya myths with her,
then Chinese and Korean legends, too.

My mind is totally blown. But Ms. Wong
is just getting started. She plays us a song:

"Bandal," which means "Half Moon,"
a slow, pretty tune from her childhood.

Gliding down the Milky Way, across the dark sky.
A little white boat carries a bunny and a tree.

The lyrics of songs, she tells us, are just poems
set to music. I'd never thought of it that way.

Then we read a poem by Miguel León-Portilla
about the moon rabbit. He wrote it in Nahuatl,

the language of the Aztecs, and the paper
has both Spanish and English translations.

I could contemplate the night birds
and the rabbit in the moon at last.

We discuss it in pairs, and Bobby Lee is so excited.
All these lit languages? In English class? Whoa!

Later, Ms. Wong says something I can't forget:
"Poetry is the clearest lens for viewing the world."

That night, I start googling the lyrics of my
favorite songs, laid out in stanzas and refrains.

She's right. It's poetry, all metaphor and rhyme,
floating on music like the moon in the sky.

From then on, Ms. Wong becomes a hero to me
as she pairs up poems from past and present,

pulling back the lid and showing us the secrets,
like how Frost's snow-filled woods symbolize death

or why Soto drops an orange, glowing like fire,
into the hands of a love-struck boy my age.

And I'm hooked. I begin to read everything
she gives me, amazing yet familiar voices,

they show me truths I recognize at once,
though I didn't know the words before.

My mind and heart swell with all the things
I need to say, and one day it just happens:

I put pen to paper, and my soul
comes rushing out in line after line.

TRICKSTER

Mr. Gil, our social studies teacher,
announces a "thematic unit" one day.
He and Ms. Wong are teaming up
to teach us about...masks.

People make masks around the world,
but we focus on Mexico and Korea.
We learn about ancient rituals,
plays, dances—and how newer traditions
blended with the old ways
and made different masks.

We read and write and reflect.
To me, the best thing is that masks
can either hide or reveal your identity.
You can pretend to be something else—
a god, a monster, a princess, a priest—
or you can show your true self,
your animal soul,
your skeleton.

For our final project, Ms. Wong
invites to class her friend, a Mexican artist
named Celeste de Maíz, expert mask-maker.
She shows us her work: crazy, awesome
faces carved from mesquite,
painted in wild colors.

Then she shows us how to make our own
from papier-mâché. I think long and hard.

Should I pretend or reveal? What's inside me?
Mr. Gil looks up my birth date. He tells me
that in the Aztec and Maya calendar
the day is 11 Dog. Any canine, he says,
might be my animal soul.

Right away, I know. The Feathered Coyote.
Aztec Trickster. God of music and mischief,
wisdom and story-telling. All decked out
with orange and gold feathers
to echo my own copper hair.

The mask is straight fire!
And los Bobbys have made some, too:
Handy's is a bright blue skull
lined with silver flowers.
Lee makes an old Korean monk
with rainbow streaks down his nose.
But Delgado blows us all away—
a carnival mask with a duckbill
and feathery horns! Savage!

That weekend, we can't resist.
These masks can't just go on our walls.
We walk out to the desert at the city's edge
wearing shorts and sneakers.
Then we strap on our masks
and run through the chaparral
chasing lizards and spiders,
playing out our secret selves
to earth and sky.

BIRTHDAY MEDLEY

My brother turns seven today.
Come listen to the joyful sounds!

Dale, dale, dale—
No pierdas el tino,
porque si lo pierdes...
Boom! The piñata explodes!

The pingos flock for the candy like crows!
Bolsitas for those who move too slow!

Estas son las mañanitas
que cantaba el rey David—
Happy birthday to you,
Happy birthday to you,
Happy birthday, Arturito...

Make a wish,
then blow!
¡Mordida!
¡Mordida!
¡Mordida!

Don't wipe the icing from your chin
till I snap a photo—come on, grin!

Give me a hug, carnalito!
Open my present primerito!

SUNDAYS

Get up early, go to mass,
get back home and cut the grass.

Take a shower, time to eat,
sit with dad to watch TV.

Read a book to stretch my brain,
then try to beat that video game.

Dinner's next, the family talks,
more TV, an evening walk.

Practice accordion in the garage,
dreaming of fans and loud applause.

Status updates, post some memes,
text my bros till moonlight gleams.

Brush my teeth and say my prayers,
close my eyes (please no nightmares).

Sundays end without a warning—
just like that, it's Monday morning!

RECORDS

Every week I walk down the street
to visit my Bisabuela Luisa.
She's almost eighty, frail and slow,
but in her heart she's lively and fun—
and she loves music!

She serves me agua de melón,
which she makes special
just for me: she knows
it's my favorite thing to drink.
We look through her records together
as she tells me about the singers
the songwriters
the orchestras
of that old
golden
age.

Like ancient heroes,
their names echo in our hearts:
Tomás Méndez Sosa
José Alfredo Jiménez
Chavela Vargas
Jorge Negrete
Pedro Infante
Lucha Reyes
Los Panchos.

With steady hands,
my great-grandmother slides
an album from its sleeve,
sets it on the turntable,
lowers the needle.
From the hiss and crackle
emerge these old-timey
but beautiful sounds.
I watch her lean back in her chair
closing her eyes,
transported to the past.

VARIEDAD MUSICAL

Though we each have different tastes,
music has a special place
in my family members' lives
so that we thrive, not just survive.

Grandpa Manuel prefers conjunto bands.
Tío Mike cranks the Tejano strand.
My great-uncle Juan finds rock 'n' roll keen.
Tía Vero thinks she's a disco queen.

My brother streams songs
from his favorite cartoons.
My sister likes reggae
and K-pop and blues.

Uncle Danny's into rap—
snare cracks, high-hat attacks,
smooth flow from a hip-hop soul,
phat synths and a low bass roll.

Dad and Joe like country tunes:
Guitars twang and voices croon
about dogs and trucks and fishing boats
or love among the creosote.

Mamá escucha rock en español
to balance her passion for classical.
I also mix both old and new—
boleros, rancheras, dub-step grooves.

En las fiestas hay variedad musical—
we respect one another and jam to it all!

LA MANO PACHONA

Just last week, between classes,
me and los Bobbys ducked into the restroom.
I needed to go so bad, but froze
at the entrance to the stall,
craning my neck, peering into the toilet.

"What the heck, Güero?" asked Bobby Delgado,
and my face went red with embarrassment.
"Fam, I'm just checking, okay?
Some guys forget to flush!"
The other Bobbys laughed.

That wasn't really the truth. I was still afraid
of a supernatural threat. Eight years ago,
my abuela Mimi told us a tale
that left a lasting mark.
I kind of deserved it.

I was the smallest back then,
sat behind my cousins as Mimi told
the scariest stories she could muster,
legends already old
when she was a little girl.

But I was mischievous for my size,
reaching out to snatch cookies
off my primos' plates as they leaned forward,
eyes wide, eagerly hanging
on every frightening word.

As I shoved galletas into my mouth,
Mimi's eyes would narrow and narrow some more,
and I could almost hear her thinking,
"You sneaky brat, huerco ladrón—
just you wait and see."

For my grandma didn't spank us,
she hardly ever raised her voice.
No, to punish little devils
she would put us in some creepy tale,
as I was about to discover.

"A new story," she announced one week,
"about la Mano Pachona." I shivered
while other boys cheered.
This legend scared me the most:
A hairy claw that crawls through the dark.

Mimi once told us the claw had belonged
to a Maya wizard who long ago
refused to renounce his people's gods.
So the Inquisition cut off all his limbs
not knowing he'd cast a spell on his left hand.

Now it seeks its revenge, waiting
for naughty boys with Spanish blood.
"Like each of you," Mimi would say
with a glint of glee in her eye
as we gulped and gasped.

On that day, she said she'd reveal
the identity of one of its victims.
"Once upon a time, there was a güerito,
sinful and travieso, who liked to steal sweets
that didn't belong to him."

My cousins giggled. They knew
what was coming. "But at last
the red-haired pingo ate his final cookie.
He swallowed that stolen, crunchy goodness
and felt his tummy rumble. Potty time.

"Up he jumped to run down the hall,
singing a foolish tune to himself:
'Ha, ha, ha—I stole your cookie!
Ha, ha, ha—you didn't catch me!'
Then he entered the bathroom.

"Shutting the door, he dropped his pants
and sat down to do his business.
But, ¡ay, pobre güerito! Big mistake.
He should've looked before he sat.
Maybe his fate would have changed.

"For there, waiting for him
deep in the water at the bottom
of the bowl...WAS LA MANO PACHONA!
It reached up and grabbed him
and pulled him into the sewer!

"He was never seen or heard from again."
My face went white as a sheet.
Just a runt, I believed her every story
was the absolute truth.
So this had to be prophecy!

"No, abuelita!" I cried, shaking,
"Don't let la Mano Pachona
grab my butt!"
You see, that was the worst thing of all.
Not being dragged away and killed, no.

I mean, let's be honest. I'd be famous!
Imagine the headlines: BORDER KID
SLAIN BY MONSTER CLAW. Yaaaas.
Immortality! But not BORDER KID
HAS BUTT GRABBED BY MONSTER CLAW.

Mimi leaned toward me as I trembled,
snot bubbling in my button nose.
"Then STOP STEALING COOKIES,
you naughty little thief!"
And so I did. Forever.

Still, there's a part of me—
foolish, I know—that can't help
but wonder if she could see the future
and if one day I'll sit down
to meet my destiny at last.

MISCHIEF

One night Handy—I use my friends' last names—
texts me to sneak out and bring my BB gun.
"Let's shoot snakes and stuff." Oh, dear God,
I actually agree. Dumbest thing I've ever done.

We walk along the alleys, the four of us,
taking shots at scurrying blurs, passing
the rifle around. Then Handy aims for a streetlight,
makes the world darker with a pull of the trigger.

There's something exciting about the effect
and we go a little nuts, each pumping the weapon
to smash another light. We laugh like hyenas,
give each other fist bumps, run to the next block.

The BB gun's back in my hands as we walk past
Don Mario's back yard, his huge sliding glass doors.
"Crack them!" Delgado urges, and I lift the barrel—
but there sits the old man in his chair, watching me.

I lower the rifle. My stomach does somersaults.
Don Mario stands, opens the doors, steps into the night.
"Córranle pa' sus casas," he says sternly. "Get on home,
boys. Ain't no reason for y'all to be prowling about."

We tramp home, silent. I keep seeing Don Mario's eyes,
his disappointment. Back in my room, I slide the rifle
under my bed. I want to forget. Let it gather dust.
I don't ever want to touch it again.

CONFESSION

I step
into the booth
to confess my sins, but
in Spanish. Father García
just sighs.
Heart beating fast, I realize
I'll never fool this priest:
He's heard (and seen)
my sins.

White lies,
copied homework,
that stolen comic book,
a certain bottle rocket blast—
chuckling,
he assigns penance in English.
"I know your voice, Güero.
God knows your heart.
Be good."

THOUGHTS AT MASS

During mass, I look around.
Most of our side of town is here,
but not my three best friends.

Handy is Mormon—his big,
loving family goes to a meetinghouse
in their ward the next city over.

Lee is Presbyterian—he prefers "Christian,"
though I remind him we Catholics are too.
His folks attend a church down the road.

Delgado doesn't belong to a religion,
though his mom says prayers to ancestors
and old gods. He told me he's agnostic.

I googled it: "Someone who thinks
it's impossible to know if God exists."
This freaked me out a little—
it's obvious to me that there's a God
because I see Him in everything around me
and feel Him in my heart.

How can Delgado doubt Him?
I spent days wondering, worrying.
Each night I prayed for los Bobbys.

We can't all be right, can we?
Three of us must be wrong—
unless...we all are. Whoa. Impossible.

Just now, Father García read from scripture:
"Do not judge, and you will not be judged;
the judgements you give are the ones you will get."

Well, that's a relief! Like an answer to prayer.
Can't wait till this afternoon—los Bobbys and me?
We're going to the movies downtown.

THE NEWCOMER

There's a new kid
in math class this week—
Andrés Palomares,
quiet and shy.
At the bell,
he slips off to ESL
so I know he must be
a newcomer,
an immigrant.

During lunch,
he eats by himself.
I leave los Bobbys
to join him.
"¿Puedo?"
I ask as I sit,
and he nods.
He doesn't say much,
but I learn he's Honduran.

Next day, I ask
Mr. García to let me
tutor Andrés.
He pairs us up.
"¿Por qué?"
the new kid asks.
I shrug. "Why not?"
And I help him read
a word problem.
A week goes by.
Andrés warms to me,

joins us at lunch,
chats with Delgado.
Until,
reading a problem
in halting English,
he whispers these words—
"A family takes a train."

Eyes red, Andrés
pushes away from the table
and runs from the room.
With Mr. García's permission,
I follow.
At last I find him,
tucked into a little alcove
near the library, crying.
"¿Qué te pasa?" I ask.

His story comes steaming out—
threats against the family,
abandoning Honduras,
risking life and limb on la Bestia,
the black train that rattles
through Mexico bottom to top.
Hopeful and dreaming of new lives,
refugees from all over cling
to that dangerous metal.
One terrible day, its wheels
sliced off his brother's leg.

"We lost everything
but each other

to coyotes and cops
and bandits,"
he says.
"Now we live in a tejabán
in a colonia. No water,
no light. But safe.
Except when I dream."

I help him stand, hug him quick.
I hadn't realized, but there's
a dozen new students
at school this year—
like Andrés
they crossed Mexico
on top of trains
through dry deserts,
sometimes without parents.

I see the worry
in their eyes:
Hunger, deportation,
school bullies.
Now Andrés and I
welcome each
with a warm smile.
Bienvenido, we say.
Welcome, friend.

CHRISTMAS CONCRETE

My father is a builder
like his father Manuel
and his father before him—
"Generaciones de albañiles,"
he says with a smile.

Over the years
he's built his own business,
a small construction company—
steady work for abuelo
and most of my tíos.

It's a family thing
so he makes me help
when school is out—
"You need an oficio,
a profession to sustain you."

This winter break,
I'm assigned to Grandpa Manuel,
plasterer by trade—
he makes me carry wet cement
like grey ice cream in a wheelbarrow.

It's cold. My hands are bleeding.
My muscles ache. I'm sleepy.
During a break, I groan—
"I hate this job. Why me?
I'm going to college, you know."

"Ya sé, m'ijo. But there's value
in manual labor, Red. Dignity, too.
Me and your apá, we got a duty—
can't let you wind up useless
with your God-given hands."

I guess he's got a point,
but believe you me,
after I get my degree,
no more Christmas concrete
for this ginger güero!

UNCLE JOE'S HISTORY LESSONS

My uncle Joe
is the family chronicler,
a cowboy philosopher,
our local expert in
Mexican American history—
he lived through a lot of it!

One day we head to the river,
set up chairs in our favorite spot,
a shady refuge at the edge of his ranch.
"When I was a chavalito," he says, watching
the water flow, "didn't nobody teach us
about our gente, about the Revolución.
They made the Treaty of Guadalupe Hidalgo
sound like a blow struck for democracy
instead of the violent land-grab it was!
This should be México, m'ijo. The border?
It crossed right over us.

"Es más, when I was in elementary
they didn't let me call myself José!
It was Joseph this and Joseph that.
So I became Joe. And forget using Spanish.
They caught you saying a single word, y
¡PAS! You got smacked."

Spellbound and angry, I ask Uncle Joe
if that's why he never went to college
even though he's so smart.

"Pos, sí. Also, nobody believed in me.
Fíjate. When I was in 7th grade like you?
Counselor asked me what I wanted to be.
A lawyer, I said. That white lady almost
laughed in my face. 'What? No, Joseph.
You should go to a technical college,
become a mechanic. No shame in
Hard work!' Vieja racista.

"Still, I kept at it, Güero. Studied hard.
But in high school? Turned in a paper
for world history about the Conquista.
I worked so hard on it, did research,
revised and edited, todo ese jale.
Know what I got? An F. I'm not kidding.
Teacher said it was too good.
Obviously plagiarized. After that, pos,
I gave up. Gatekeepers weren't letting
this Chicano through."

Then he leans forward and looks
at me, super serious, his eyes suddenly red
with rage or sadness or hope.
Even the chachalacas go quiet,
like they're listening, too.
"Don't you let them stop you, chamaco.
Push right through them gates.
It's your right. You deserve a place
at that table. But when you take your seat,
don't let it change you. Represent us, m'ijo,
all the ones they kept down. You are us.
We are you."

TAMALADA

Christmas Eve Day, we gather at Mimi's house,
excited to make dozens of warm tamales.
Usually the women and girls do the work
while the men watch football. Not this year!
Teresa, my tomboy sister, wants to see the game,
so I take her place, happy with my small job
of soaking the cornhusks in water.
I love the gossip, el chisme!

Mimi kneads the masa, of course, correcting
everyone with a scolding voice though her eyes
are full of mischief. My mother and her concuñas
cook the fillings: chicken, beans, pork, sweet raisins.
Aunt Vero and my cousins Silvia and Magy spread
a thin layer of dough on cornhusks with silver spoons.
"Careful!" Mimi calls. "Those are family heirlooms,
last bit of wealth from before la Revolución!"

Other teams of tías and primas spoon in
the fillings, fold them up, tie them tight,
and stand them neat in pots for baño maría steaming.
The warmth of the kitchen mixes with laughter
as great-grandma Luisa stirs the champurrado,
and leads the rich plática: stories, gossip,
old dichos that make us laugh with happiness
nourishing us like good tamales!

"You know, muchachas," she announces, grinning,
"Jorge never tried to kiss me when we were a-courtin'.

As God is my witness. I kept giving him hints, pero nada.
Well, after a while, I got good and fed up. Took matters
into my own hands back behind his father's barn."
All the women burst into laughter, and I try to picture
my great-grandfather Don Jorge as an awkward boy.
"A bit dense, these men," Luisa adds with a wink.

Mimi pulls a fist from the masa and gestures.
"Like father, like son...con todo respeto,"
she says to her suegra. "A fact y'all may not know:
Manuel always cheats on his golf score.
He figures nobody's noticed his handicap."
Silvia frowns, annoyed. "And you don't tell him
anything, abuela?" Mimi laughs. "Ay, m'ija.
What good would it do? I just let him win!"

Mom chimes in at once. "Oh, and when he
and his son get together! Güero, do you remember
when your grandpa Manuel and your dad
went deep-sea fishing? Well, they didn't catch a thing."
My mouth falls open. "But...we ate those fillets!"
Mom shakes her head. "That's because they bought
a swordfish from a beachside store. Then they lied,
said they'd reeled it in by themselves!"

My little cousin Silvia turns to me. "Hey, didn't
Grandpa Manny put beer in your bottle
when you were a baby?" I shake off some husks
and reply. "Yup, but I squirted that nasty stuff
right in his eye!" The women all nod in approval.

"Cada hombre cuerdo lleva un loco dentro,"
mutters Tía Susana. "There's a nutjob waiting
inside every sane man!" They all agree.

Tía Vero, laughing, jumps in next. "On the day
of our wedding, Mike backed his car into a ditch,
remember? We were already running so late."
Mimi groans. "Ah, sí. His brothers had to lift it out.
Ese Mike, always in danger. You know what they say:
Arrimarse a la boca del lobo, es de hombre bobo.
Our men dive right into the jaws of the wolf!
What lovely fools."

Luisa looks at me and shakes her head.
"Speak of the devil. Los hombres y las gallinas,
poco tiempo en la cocina, Güerito. Go on,
check the score. My Cowboys best be winning!"
I head to the living room, hear encouraging cheers,
think about the gossip I've heard. It might sound
mean, but it's just for fun. They love us, their men and
boys, warts and all.

After the game, the whole clan sits down to eat,
smiling and hungry, offering prayers and replays.
The tamales are more delicious than ever,
bursting with flavor, full of rich fillings, sure,
but also so much history,
hard work, great fun,
and family magic.

FOOD FOR EACH SEASON

EIGHT HAIKU

San Marcos blanket—
only the sound of bacon
can make me emerge.

Sipping atole,
folks search their piece of rosca
for baby Jesus.

Hazy spring morning—
stopping for breakfast tacos
on the way to school.

South Padre Island
teeming with college students,
the warm Gulf with shrimp.

Fragrant white flowers
on a sea of glossy green—
Red Ruby grapefruit.

The smell of pizza
in the hallways of my school—
summer's almost here.

Cold and juicy red—
the watermelon awaits
its chile dusting.

White-hot, pitiless,
the sun bakes the earth bone-dry…
where's the raspa man?

THE GIFT

This whole semester I've moaned and groaned,
"All of my friends have got a cell phone!"
while I begged my parents for one of my own.

"You're way too young," my mom calmly said.
"They're way too expensive," added my dad,
"It would put our budget far into the red!"

Grandpa Manny argued they make kids lazy.
Abuela declared I would drive her crazy:
Eyes glued to the screen, sight going hazy.

No phone till high school begins, it seems.
But as presents pile up under the tree,
I examine each bag and box carefully.

A daily ritual until Christmas morning,
when we rip off the wrapping in front of adoring
adults. I'm a bit disappointed until, without warning,

Dad hands me a gift that fits in my palm,
I tear the thing open, forgetting all calm.

It's a cheap pulga knock-off, but I do not groan—
I hug both my parents, shouting,
"Thanks for the phone!"

ANSWERING THE BULLY

First I hear
Snake's voice.
"Think you're all that,
güero cacahuatero?"
Then his hand
grabs my head,
slams me into a locker.

I stumble, turn.
"What the—?"
He sneers at me
and everybody
in the hallway
laughs.
"Fancy house,
teacher's pet,
stupid poems,
all these freckles—
you're just a gringo nerd."

I can't think.
The bell's about to ring.
I rush to class.
Ms. Wong frowns
at the red blotch
on my face.
My friends whisper
encouragement,
but my ears are
full of rage.

He's too big,
too mean,
too ignorant.
I yank out
my journal
and answer Snake
with words
instead of fists.
Ms. Wong watches,
concern on her face,
as I scratch
furiously.
And when her timer
dings
she asks me to
stand and read.

> Yo, bullies: lero, lero
> I'm the mero Güero
> a real cacahuatero,
> peanuts and chile
> all up in this cuero,
> this piel, this skin—
> it's white, that's true
> but I'm just as Mexican
> as you and you and you.

My voice shakes
but I meet their eyes.
In the back,
Snake's friend

El Chaparro
shakes his head,
puts his phone away.
He's recorded
every word.

I head for my seat.
Bobby Lee bumps my fist
before whispering
"That was lit,
but he's gonna kill you."

Probably.
Still, it felt good
to stand my ground
and clap back
with rap.

JOANNA LA FREGONA

Even when I was a little boy
still thinking girls were gross,
Abuela Mimi gave me romantic advice:

"Find yourself a fregona, Güerito,
a tough one who doesn't need you at all
but wants you anyway.
Así como María Félix o Frida Kahlo,
a woman who will be your companion,
your equal in life and love."

Now I know what she meant.

There's a girl in my social studies class,
Joanna Padilla. Can't get her off my mind.
She's kind of pretty, but that's not
what matters to me.

She's smart and rude,
takes judo classes after school,
helps her dad in his body shop,
loves superhero films and video games.
Okay, I'm a little obsessed, I'll admit.
But I have zero luck. When I ask her
to be my girlfriend, she just laughs.

I even write her a long poem,
which she just sticks in her back pocket
like a restroom pass. Nothing works!

After school that bully Snake Barrera
decides to rearrange my face, just as
Joanna goes walking by. "Help me!"
I call. "Help me, Joanna." She turns
and tells him to leave me alone.

When he laughs and tries to hit me again,
she grabs his arm and throws him down.

"Took guts to ask a girl for help,"
Joanna says as she pulls me to my feet.
"I liked your poem. Funny and sweet.
Okay, Güero. You can be my boyfriend."

I wipe blood from my lip
as the kids who've gathered
Go "ooh" and "aah."
Then my fregona smiles.

"You got any money?
We can go to Rosy's.
Fighting makes me hungry."

NEIGHBORHOODS

When school's out each day
I walk home with my bros and girl,
stopping at Rosy's Drive-Thru
for Takis preparados
and agua mineral.

There, Handy's mom
picks him up in her hybrid.
Like all the older families,
they live closer
to the heart of town.
Sometimes Lee catches a ride with them
to his family's store.

The rest of us keep walking.
Andrés peels off toward the south,
waving goodbye
as he enters his colonia—
caliche streets, mobile homes,
wooden shacks.
His dogs rush to greet him.

Rising slow across the street
come cinderblock shells of houses,
partly finished and partially roofed,
promised futures looming.

Joanna squeezes my hand
and heads that way with Delgado
licking Taki dust off her fingers.

A subdivision
sprawls a little farther down—
big residences
bought ready-made by families
who come with plenty of cash.
On days when Lee has piano practice,
he slaps me on the back
and hurries along those well-paved streets,
past manicured lawns
to his parents' fancy home.

Our house, though,
stands by itself,
on a half-acre lot
in the shade of mesquite,
ebony, anacua trees.
I pause on the porch
and look back up the road.

We were one of the first families
here on the northernmost side.
Dad helped build a bunch
of these neighborhoods

as new moms and dads arrived
from Mexico and even further south.
Everyone works hard, tries to make
a better life for their families.
I feel safe on these caliche streets,
among these humble houses—
I hear little kids laughing
in the distance
and I smile.

VALENTINE TEXTS

me:

bae u want roses
or candy for valentines?
im shopping for something nice

her:

roses die, wero
candy gives me zits. mejor
hold my hand, write me a poem

MOVIES

We've got a plan.
One Saturday me and los Bobbys
get dropped off at the movies
by our parents.
Joanna's already there
with three of her cousins.
We buy popcorn and coke.
My friends make stupid jokes.
The girls just roll their eyes and giggle.
We grab seats in a middle row:
Boys on the left, girls on the right,
me and Joanna in the middle.

The plan is working perfectly.
At least for me. Los Bobbys?
They keep stealing glances,
but Joanna's cousins
act like they don't notice
my weird and desperate friends.

The movie takes forever to start.
Fifteen minutes of commercials,
followed by trailers that spoil
all the cool scenes and jokes
of the spring's big releases.
Finally the lights dim.
It's the latest superhero film.

I try to pay attention
but it's not all that intense.
Besides, I feel Joanna's presence
like electricity crackling beside me.
A moment of suspense comes—
she jumps, grabs my hand.
Our fingers lock and the film fades.

All I can think about is the pressure
of her arm against mine,
the scent of her hair
as she leans against me,
putting her head on my shoulder.

Then the credits roll.
The lights come on.
We untangle ourselves,
and I feel a little weird.
Me and Joanna,
we don't look at each other.

But somehow each boy
is sitting next to a girl!
How did that happen?

I laugh with los Bobbys.
Joanna talks with her cousins.
We all try to act
like nothing has changed.

REMEDIOS Y RAREZAS

SUPERSTITIOUS SENRYU

Me and los Bobbys
compare all the strange beliefs
our families share.

Red rags around chair legs
so tricky little devils
don't make moms forget.

If you hiccup,
Abuelita licks a red thread,
sticks it to your forehead.

For the worst migraines,
rolling an egg on your head
takes away the pain.

Sweep a girl's feet
and she'll never get married—
my sister grabs the broom!

When nothing goes right,
bundles of burning sage
drive bad vibes away.

Chamomile tea
(to judge from how much we drink)
must cure everything.

At dinner tables,
you never pass the salt—
it's just bad luck.

My tías' purses
have never touched the floor—
they think they'll go broke.

I wore red chones
on New Year's—a gift from Mom.
Love was on its way!

CASCARÓN WAR

After Easter Mass,
we head to Tía Vero's house
to hunt for bright eggs
amid blooming citrus trees.

Half-acre dotted
with specks of vibrant color:
Huercos rush with joy,
baskets swinging in their hands.

Some eggs are plastic,
stuffed with candy, jangling coins.
I want the others,
los cascarones!

These are the true prizes!
Hollowed out, confetti-filled
or heavy with flour,
sealed with tape and loud pastels.

Cousins jostle me,
competing for this ammo,
these small gaudy bombs
we collect in plastic bags.

Even young uncles
snatch a few from little kids
and the war is on
like mock combats in ancient times.
Teresa gets me,

smashes the shell on my head
rainbow dandruff falls,
but I don't chase her. Patience.

Instead, I lob eggs
at Joseph and Álvaro,
duck down so pingos
like Arturo can reach me.

I crack a pink shell
in the air over mom's hair
(would never hit her)
and let vivid fragments fall.

The yard's a riot
of squeals and screams and laughter.
Little bits of construction paper
drift among the flowers.

I see my sister. Time for payback!
I stalk her like a hunter,
keeping out of sight,
circling behind the grapefruit trees.

I heft the flour-packed cascarón,
sneaking up behind her, then
CRASH! against her cranium:
Dust her ghost-white in revenge.

LA LECHUZA OUTSIDE MY WINDOW

Last night I stayed up late
watching a horror movie on my tablet.
It was hard to get to sleep—
I lay there tossing and turning
for a while, squeezing my eyes shut,
but the moonlight streaming in
was too bright on my face,
so I got up, sighing, to close the blinds.

There,
on a thick limb
of the mesquite tree
just outside my window,
perched the biggest lechuza
I have ever seen, a bone-white
screech owl with inky black eyes
and demon-horn tufts high on its head,
which swiveled toward me at that very moment.

I could hear Mimi's voice
echoing in my fluttering heart:
"Not all lechuzas are simple owls, Güerito.
Some are witches in disguise
using the cover of feathers and darkness
to carry out bad deeds. Así que ojo,
be on your guard. If it stares, not blinking,

then lets loose a horrible screech,
it might be the end of you!"
I don't believe her legends anymore,
I'm not a little kid, shivering in fear
that a witch owl could come crashing
through the window, into my room,
and fly away with me in its talons.

But still
I thought,
why tempt fate?

I closed the blinds,
drew the curtains shut,
and got back under the covers.

Now I struggled even more
to drift off, but finally I did,
Durmiendo con los angelitos.
Till I woke up with a start
around 3 am,
covered in sweat,
panting,
the screech of an owl
echoing in my ears.

I leaped from bed
and pulled back the curtains
of the south window,

peering through the blinds.
Nothing.
I laughed weakly
at my own foolishness
and turned back to bed.
That's when I saw it,
silhouetted against the curtains
of the west window,
the one with no blinds at all.

The owl had flown to a different tree,
sat there in silence, staring at me.

Without hesitation, I grabbed my pillow
and my blanket, hurried down the hall
to my little brother's room
and squeezed beside him on that narrow bed.

It's strange how safe
another person's presence makes us feel.
He couldn't do a thing to stop the owl,
but his gentle breathing calmed my fear.

I closed my tired eyes at last,
glad to be next to my little brother.
Better to be safe than sorry, I thought
as I fell back into deep sleep.

BALLAD OF THE MIGHTY TLACUACHE

The big opossum clambered down
the knotted old mesquite;
as night had fallen thick and dark,
it was now time to eat.

The humans' garbage can was close,
he followed that sweet smell.
But then he caught the briefest whiff
of evil scents as well—

The prowling cat, his nemesis!
Invader of this land!
Whose ancestors had crossed the sea
along with the white man!

It leapt into the space between
Tlacuache and his meal;
it arched its back and puffed its fur
and gave a hissing squeal.

Opossum bared his pointed teeth,
and curled his agile tail:
A growl began deep in his chest
soon rising to a wail.

The tomcat pounced and batted hard
with two soft-padded paws.
What made his enemy retreat
were those sharp, dirty claws.

The cat moved in to sink its teeth
below that wedge-shaped head.
But old Tlacuache reeled in pain
and promptly just dropped dead.

The back door opened, lights came on.
The tomcat's owner called.
Reluctantly, it strolled away
from where the corpse lay sprawled.

But once the night was dark again,
that big opossum moved.
With nimble hands and agile tail,
he searched the trash for food.

That's why this mighty 'possum
is so hard to combat:
For even with his puny brain,
he's smarter than a cat.

PLAYOFF GAME

All pumped, we board the spirit bus—
my sister's team has made the cut!
Now nearly our entire town
is heading north. We're playoff bound!

We fill the stands around the court
and cheer the girls as they transport
that ball with skill right toward the hoop—
a leap, a swoosh, we stand and whoop!

Before too long we're in the lead.
The other fans now boo and scream
and then a sickening chant commences
horrible words that beat at our senses.

"Go back, wetbacks! Build that wall!"
Adults and teens begin to call.
A sea of white faces, twisting in rage
like all the brown bodies are there to invade.

Teresa my sister stops dead in her tracks.
We're shocked as well at this ugly attack.
We're Americans too! This just isn't right.
My friends and I are raring to fight.

The coach asks for calm and calls a time-out:
The team huddles close, then breaks with a shout!
Heads held high, they struggle to win
despite all the hatred, despite all the din.

We fans wave banners and chant our cheers.
Together we swallow disgust and fears
to urge those ladies to sweet victory,
a game to add to our town's history.

When all is over, the other team's coach
asks our forgiveness in front of the crowd.
Security clears us a path to our vehicles
and we march off together, proud and unbeatable.

"Next up: state champs!" We chant on the bus,
convinced that once more we'll be victorious.
If not, no worries, it's the team's finest hour—
we'll put this win on our town's water tower.

SPANISH BIRDS

Everyone I know
speaks a different Spanish:
The rural twang of border folk,
the big-city patter of immigrants,
the shifting mix of Tex-Mex.

Sometimes we laugh
at each other;
sometimes we just listen
in awe at the sweet sounds
that leave our lips
like birds taking flight.

Mom's Spanish flits around
like a hummingbird—
a fast and frantic blur of color
delicate dancing perfection.

Dad's is like a swan—
ugly and awkward at first,
but growing into something beautiful,
comfortable in both water and air.

Delgado's Dominican accent
reminds me of flamingos—
stepping high to avoid every "s,"
beaks making each "r" liquid.

Handy's Spanglish is like an ostrich—
flightless and a little clumsy,
yet still pretty powerful
and fast when it gets going.

I hear the echo of their calls
when I speak.
My own tongue
is an aviary.

MIS OTROS ABUELOS

Once every couple of months or so
and most spring breaks as well,
we leave Puchi at the ranch:
My parents pack our bags
and we take a bus
to Monterrey,
Nuevo León,
México.

Get out
at the bridge,
walk through inspection.
Then an hour later, at the garita,
agents and soldiers come on board—
they never ask for our papers though.
I guess we look Mexican enough for them.

Me and my brother nap almost all the way,
till our sister nudges us awake.
We're close to the city—
the mountains
are looming.

Mom's parents,
mis otros abuelos,
are always waiting at the station,
and they squeeze us with papacho hugs.

There's a room set up for us at their house
and all our favorite food, prepared
by Mamá Toñita's expert hands.
She makes limonada,
hands me glorias
when no one's
looking.

Then,
after we've eaten,
Tata Moncho takes us boys
on some adventure with our primos,
to a park or waterfall, some outdoor stuff.
We play and joke about Arturo's pocho Spanish.

Every day there's something to do in Monterrey.
It's a big, sprawling city with lots of history.
It's also part of me. When we leave,
me siento recargado de cultura
more Mexican, I suppose,
with the gentle kisses
of my other abuelos
on my forehead
like lucky charms
against all
harm.

WEDDING IN MONTERREY

My mom's sister Pilar
is getting married.
We're gathered
in a chapel
in Apodaca
right outside
Monterrey,
dressed formal
for just this once
as the priest intones
such serious words.
Vows exchanged,
rings fitted tight,
the novios kneel
on little pillows
and get lassoed
with lazos of love.

Then caravan
to a reception hall
for the real draw—
la pachanga.
Bottles and fancy
centerpieces
at each table,
cake towering.

My cousins and I
play outside till
the food is served.
Then I stay in my seat
to watch my aunt
and new uncle dance
El Vals de Novios,
which isn't a waltz
but is beautiful
all the same.

¡Se abre la pista!
Couples young
and old get up,
moving to the rhythm
of cumbias.
After a bit
everyone halts
and lifts a glass
¡Brindis!
Cake is shared,
bouquet thrown,
then the men
heft the groom
into the air—
¡Muertito!—
while a funeral march
marks the passing
of his bachelorhood.

Everyone laughs,
la fiesta sigue,
till the newlyweds
drive away
and the guests head home,
admiring the recuerdos
we each get
to keep.

LOSING PUCHI

Pregnant with me, Mom was watering plants
when a scrawny puppy crawled its way
to her feet and just lay there,
like it was surrendering at last.
She nursed it back to health,
named it Puchi.

From the moment I got home as a baby,
Puchi was there. She was a good dog,
guarding me day and night.
When I learned to walk,
it was with my hand on her head
as she guided my steps.

I grew. She grew faster, more mature
and cautious, but always eager to play.
Together we explored el barrio
y el monte, walking all the way down
to the resaca and back again,
a boy and his best friend.

Puchi was loyal to my family and fierce,
ready to protect us, no matter what.
Once my mom pulled into the driveway,
started to get out of her truck—
but there, snarling and angry,
was the neighbors' pit bull,
escaped from its yard.

Mom screamed in fear, slamming the door!
Then, her teeth bared in a growl,
Puchi came dashing from behind the house!
WHAM! She collided with the other dog,
clamped her jaws around his thick neck,
wrestled him to the ground,
and held him there till my mom
could get Mr. Rivera,
the pit bull's owner.

Yeah, Puchi was something else.
She was magnificent.
She was.
Was.

Her brown muzzle was showing white
when I entered middle school,
but I figured we still had many years.
I prayed each night that she be safe
that I make it to college before the end.
Maybe adulthood
would keep my heart
from breaking.

But I walked home one afternoon
and saw blood
in a strange spiral
around our home.
My gut twisted.

Dropping my books,
I rushed to the back yard
and found her
lying beneath a mesquite tree,
her face peaceful
as if in sleep.

Later, as we stood over her grave,
my hands and heart aching,
tears streaming down my face,
I told my dad, "She circled the house
three times before she died. Ah, Puchi,
your last thought was to keep us safe."

Even now
months later
I miss my dog.
I miss my friend.
Good girl, Puchi.
Good girl.

WHEELS

Tío Dan loves his lowrider—
candy apple red and mint green,
thirteen-inch whitewalls, wire-spoke rims,
it dominates car shows.

Uncle Joe drives his pickup truck
all over his ranch, hauling hay
and fenceposts and sometimes a calf.
He can't work without it.

Mom prefers her compact sedan,
great gas mileage, low emissions,
just enough room for her three kids—
our dad can squeeze in too.

Mimi has her black Oldsmobile.
"Like a hearse," she morbidly jokes.
It's ancient, yes, but with few miles—
to church and back, that's all.

Their wheels all fit them to a tee...
I wonder what my car will be.
My sister laughs. "You're such a nerd—
you'll go for a hybrid!"

CARNE ASADA

It's a ritual—
Dad sends me out to collect
twigs and small branches.
He arranges them
over balled-up newspaper,
adds mesquite charcoal,
and lights the newspaper's edge.
With a little wind,
it's blazing hot in seconds.
When the heat's just right,
we clean the grill with onion.
Mom brings out the meat—
fajita and loaded ribs.
Dad opens a beer,
sips and douses rebel flames.
We put on some jams,
sometimes relatives arrive
bringing drinks on ice,
wolfing down quesadillas.
Happy fellowship
fills the air with smoke and laughs.

Inside, Mom and Sis
and whoever else is there
make guacamole,
potato salad and beans,
along with spicy pico.

The table is set,
all the sizzling meat
and lip-smacking sides
are piled high
there in the middle.
Smiling, I say a quick grace,
then everybody digs in.

FATHER'S DAY

Not embarrassed to say
that I love my dad.
Always have.
He's kind of my hero.

Mom says that when I saw him
for the first time
as a baby,
I reached my little hand up
and motioned him closer
with my wrinkled fingers.

My first word
was "papá."

When I started walking,
he would take me with him
Saturday mornings
to have an early breakfast
in town or across the border.
When we'd come home,
I'd walk through the door
by his side,
all proud and serious,
and Mom would smile,
whispering, "Mis dos hombres."

He has taught me so much,
shared the comics he collected
when he was a boy,
showed me how to hammer a nail,
fire a gun,
treat others with dignity,
be a man.

So when the third Saturday
of June rolls around,
I don't just get him a silly tie
or some other thoughtless gift—
I plan a day of Dad activities!

His favorite action films,
those spicy enmoladas
that he loves to eat,
a woodworking project
that we can do together,
tickets to some game
that I'll sit through,
cheering when he cheers,
just to make him as happy
as he makes me.

This year, when we come home from the fun,
exhausted, he hugs me and thanks me
before heading to spend time
with Teresa and Arturo.
(Their gifts are never quite as good,
but he's their dad too.)

In my room, I pick up my phone
(I left it behind
so I wouldn't be distracted),
and there are five missed calls
from Bobby Delgado.

My chest hurts a little,
looking at his name
on that screen.
I know why he's called.
Father's Day is hard on him,
means something very different,
something cruel.

Four years ago,
Delgado's dad kissed him goodbye
in the early morning hours.
He was a truck driver, Mr. Delgado.
Said he'd be back in a couple of days.

But he never returned.
The days stretched into weeks.
Delgado's mother grew desperate,
called police,
hospitals,
her husband's boss.

Mr. Delgado was gone.
He had dropped off his truck
and simply disappeared.
No explanation.
No nothing.

To this day, no one's sure
if he returned
to the Dominican Republic
or started another life
elsewhere
without the son
who bears his name—
Roberto Delgado, Jr.

Now every year,
as I hang out
with my awesome dad,
my friend suffers,
alone,
sad.

What can I do?
I call him back.
"Hey, Delgado. 'Sup?
Want to play Overwatch together?"

We both log on,
select our heroes,
help our team accomplish a goal,
shouting through our headsets,
laughing and cursing.

For a while, at least,
Delgado forgets the hole in his heart.

TERESA'S QUINCEAÑERA WALTZ

My sister Teresa
doesn't want a quinceañera,
hates dresses and dancing,
would rather get a car.

But my mom insists
because it's family tradition.
So Teresa relents
though with one firm condition:
"I want Güero to play
when the band strikes up my waltz."

Wow! I don't know what to say.
I never knew she was listening
when I practiced on and on.
I just give her a nervous thumbs-up.

Out of so many possible songs,
her pick is "Blue Danube."
Mom grins at the classical choice.
Each day on my accordion
I practice that stately tune
while Teresa rehearses
the intricate steps,
the elegant moves.
The day my sister turns fifteen,

I wait for my cue and take the stage
as she takes my father's hand,
beautiful in that dress.
My fingers glide in time with the band
and the two of them dance
as if alone in the world,
a man recognizing his daughter
for the woman she's become.

The song winds down,
the final notes sound,
and she lifts her crowned head
to catch my eye—
my big sister,
face beaming with joy,
gives me a smile.

A SONNET FOR JOANNA

If you should need a bully beaten up,
Joanna is the girl you need to call.
She'll dump the meanest tough guy on his rump
with a judo throw, like the "shoulder wheel."

The family car requires an oil change?
She'll crawl under the motor with a pan.
and if they blow a tire on the way,
she'll swap it with the spare in nothing flat.

Your team of friends can't beat that online game?
Make her a member and you'll win the match.
When spicing up the way your munchies taste,
she knows the perfect chile for all snacks.

But best of all, when it's just her and me,
Joanna is as sweet as girls can be.

THE REFUGE ON THE RANCH

It's quiet here except for the hushed flow of the river
and the hum of bugs answered by the sharp trill of birds.
Somewhere, an ocelot growls.

I know poetry when I hear it.

GLOSSARY

Abuela [ah-WEL-ah] grandmother

Abuelo [ah-WEL-oh] grandfather

Agua de melón [AH-wah theh meh-LOHN] a drink made from canteloupe

Agua mineral [AH-wah mee-neh-RAL] mineral water

Apá [ah-PAH] "pops," shortened form of papá or "father"

Así como [ah-SEE KOH-moh] just like

Así que ojo [ah-SEE keh OH-hoh] so watch out

Atole [ah-TOH-leh] hot drink made from corn starch

Baño maría [BAHN-yoh mah-REE-ah] steaming food in a pot

Bienvenido [byen-beh-NEE-thoh] welcome

Bisabuela [bee-sahb-WEL-ah] great grandmother

Brindis [BREEN-dees] a toast

Bolsitas [bol-SEE-tahs] bags of candy given out at birthday parties

Cacahuatero [kah-kah-wah-TEH-roh] someone who likes, eats, or sells peanuts

Café de olla [kah-FEH theh OH-yah] coffee with cinnamon, made in a clay pot

Canelo [kah-NEL-oh] "cinnamon-colored," the nickname of Mexican boxer Saúl Álvarez

Carnalito [kar-nah-LEE-toh] little brother

Carne asada [KAR-neh ah-SAH-thah] barbecue

Carrizo [kar-REE-soh] reeds

Cascarón [kas-kah-ROHN] hollowed-out egg shell filled with something else, like confetti

Cerveza [ser-BEH-sa] beer

Chachalaca [chah-chah-LAH-kah] a sort of noisy bird

Chafo [CHAH-foh] cheap, knock-off

Chamaco [chah-MAH-koh] boy

Champurrado [cham-poo-RAH-thoh] a chocolate drink with corn meal in it

Chavalito [chah-bah-LEE-toh] little dude

Chisme [CHEEZ-meh] gossip

Chones [CHOH-nes] undies (slang for "calzones" or "underwear")

Colonia [koh-LOH-nyah] neighborhood, often a poor one (in the US)

Con todo respeto with all due respect

Concuña [kohn-KOO-nyah] a kind of sister-in-law: the wife of the brother of a person's spouse

Córranle pa' sus casas hurry on back to your houses

Cucuy/Cucu [koo-KOO-ee] bogeyman, monster

Cuero [KWEH-roh] leather or skin

Dale [DAH-leh] hit it

Dichos [DEE-chos] traditional sayings

Durmiendo con los angelitos sleeping with the little angels

En las fiestas hay variedad musical At our parties there's musical variety

Es más what's more

Estas son las mañanitas these are the morning songs

Fíjate [FEE-hah-teh] check this out

Fregona [freh-GO-nah] tough girl

Fronterizo [frohn-teh-REE-soh] person from the border

Galleta [gah-YEH-tah] cookie

Garita [gah-REE-tah] border inspection station

Generaciones de albañiles generations of construction workers

Gente [HEN-teh] people

Glorias a type of caramel candy

Güero [WEH-roh] person with pale skin

Huerco ladrón [WER-koh lah-DROHN] thieving little brat

Huerquitos [wer-KEE-tos] young kids

Joya [HOH-yah] a Mexican brand of fruit-flavored soft drinks

La fiesta sigue the party continues

Lazos [LAH-sos] cords used in weddings to join bride and groom

Lechuza [leh-CHOO-sah] screech owl or (more commonly) a witch that has turned into one

Lero, lero a taunting cry that kids use, like "nanny nanny boo boo"

Limonada [lee-moh-NAH-thah] lemonade

Los hombres y las gallinas, poco tiempo en la cocina men and chickens should spend little time in the kitchen

Mamá escucha rock en español Mom listens to rock sung in Spanish

Me siento recargado de cultura I feel recharged with culture

Mero main one, boss, best

M'ijo [MEE-hoh] my son

Mis dos hombres my two men

Mis otros abuelos my other grandparents

Monte [MOHN-teh] woods or wild area

Muchachas [moo-CHAH-chahs] girls

Muchachos traviesos, se van a lastimar Naughty boys, you're going to hurt yourselves

Muertito [mwer-TEE-toh] little dead man

Nagual [nah-WAL] shapeshifter

No pierdas el tino don't miss when you swing

No sé I don't know

Novios [NOH-byohs] bride and groom (or girlfriend and boyfriend)

Oficio [oh-FEES-yoh] trade, occupation, profession

Pachanga [pah-CHAHN-gah] big party

Papacho [pah-PAH-choh] loving cuddle
Papeles [pah-PEL-es] papers
Para hacernos un hogar to make a home for ourselves
Pecas [PEH-kahs] freckles
Pero nada but nothing
Piel [pyel] skin or leather
Pingo [PEEN-goh] little devil, brat
Plática [PLAH-tee-kah] conversation
Pobre güerito poor little pale-skinned kid
Pocho [POH-choh] not quite Mexican, not quite American (potentially insulting)
¿Por qué? Why?
Porque si lo pierdes because if you miss [when you swing]
Pos filler word like "uh" or "well"
Pos, sí well, yeah
Prima/o cousin
Primerito [pree-meh-REE-toh] first
¿Puedo? [PWEH-thoh] Can I?
Pulga [POOL-gah] flea market
Que cantaba el rey David that King David sang
¿Qué te pasa? What's wrong with you?
Quinceañera [keen-seh-ahn-YEH-rah] a girl who is turning 15; also the big birthday party she gets
Rarezas [rah-REH-sahs] weird things
Raspa [RAHS-pah] shaved ice with flavored syrup
Recuerdos [reh-KWER-thohs] memories or mementos
Remedios [reh-METH-yohs] remedies
Resaca [reh-SAH-kah] oxbow lake
Restorán [res-toh-RAHN] restaurant
Revolución [reh-boh-loos-YOHN] revolution
Rosca [ROHS-kah] circular cake

Se abre la pista [seh AH-breh la PEES-tah] the dance-floor is open

Suegra [SWEH-grah] mother-in-law

Takis preparados [TAH-kees preh-pah-RAH-thohs] a spicy snack

Tamalada [tah-mah-LAH-thah] a gathering of loved ones to make tamales for a special occasion while having conversation.

Tejabán [teh-hah-BAHN] cheaply made wooden house

Tía [TEE-ah] aunt

Tío [TEE-oh] uncle

Tlacuache [tahk-WAH-cheh] opossum

Todo ese jale [TOH-thoh EH-seh HAH-leh] all that stuff

Travieso [trahb-YEH-soh] naughty

Ya sé I already know.

Vieja racista [BYEH-hah rah-SEES-tah] racist old lady

ABOUT THE AUTHOR

DAVID BOWLES grew up and lives in the Río Grande Valley of South Texas. A many-faceted writer and scholar, he's the author of *Feathered Serpent, Dark Heart of Sky: Myths of Mexico*. His middle-grade fantasy *The Smoking Mirror* was selected as a 2016 Pura Belpré Author Honor by the American Library Association. @DavidOBowles is active in the #weneeddiversebooks and #ownvoices movements. He's a professor at UTRGV.

CPSIA information can be obtained
at www.ICGtesting.com
Printed in the USA
JSHW020911151119
2442JS00001B/1

First edition.

THEY CALL ME GÜERO